The New Adventures of
MARY-KATE & ASHLEY™

The Case Of The
SURPRISE CALL™

The Case Of The
SURPRISE CALL™

by Melinda Metz

DUALSTAR PUBLICATIONS PARACHUTE PRESS

SCHOLASTIC INC.

New York   Toronto   London   Auckland   Sydney

DUALSTAR PUBLICATIONS TM   PARACHUTE PRESS

Dualstar Publications
c/o Thorne and Company
1801 Century Park East
Los Angeles, CA 90067

Parachute Press
156 Fifth Avenue
Suite 325
New York, NY 10010

Published by Scholastic Inc.

With special thanks to Robert Thorne and Harold Weitzberg.

Printed in the U.S.A.
February 1999
ISBN: 0-590-29403-2
A B C D E F G H I J

1

DETECTIVE HEADQUARTERS!

"**W**e're about to hang out with the best detectives in the business!" I said to my twin sister, Ashley.

"I know!" Ashley said. "And we're related to one of them!"

Our great-grandma Olive is one of the best detectives in the world. And she invited Ashley and me to spend spring break at her new detective clubhouse! The clubhouse was in Santa Fe, New Mexico. We were on our way there from the airport in a taxicab.

Most kids probably wouldn't want to spend their vacation visiting their great-grandmother and her friends. But our great-grandma Olive is the coolest. And so are her friends.

Like her best friend, Henrietta. She isn't a detective, but she makes the best chocolate-chip cookies in the world. And Zachary Ogden—he was on the cover of *Detective* magazine last month. And Bobbi and Baby Butterworth—twins *and* detectives, just like me and Ashley!

But unlike Bobbi and Baby, who look alike *and* think alike, Ashley and I just look alike. Other than that, we're totally different. Ashley's logical and likes to think things through. I like to jump right into things!

But Ashley and I always agree on one thing—we love being detectives!

"This is it, girls," the taxi driver said to us, "125 Mayfair Lane."

I stared out the window—and my mouth dropped open. "Are you sure this is the right

house?" I asked the cabdriver.

"Yup," he said.

Ashley and I got out of the cab and stared at the giant stone building in front of us. "It's a castle!" Ashley exclaimed.

"A *huge* castle!" I said as the cabdriver got our suitcases out of the trunk.

"Mary-Kate! Ashley!" called a familiar voice. Great-grandma Olive stood in the doorway of the castle, waving.

Her long, gray hair was braided and tied with a purple scrunchie at the end. I loved the fuzzy purple sweater she wore—and I think we had on the same brand of jeans!

Ashley and I both waved back, grabbed our suitcases, and ran up the wide stone steps to the castle. Great-grandma Olive gave us each a big hug.

"I'm so happy you're both here!" she said to us. "The other detectives are, too. We're thrilled that the famous Trenchcoat Twins will be guests at our Detective of the Year banquet

tomorrow night!"

Great-grandma Olive led us inside and down a long hall. Her sneakers squeaked on the polished marble floor. "What do you two think of our new detective headquarters?" Great-grandma Olive asked.

"Awesome!" Ashley said. We both stared at the curving marble staircase and glittering chandeliers.

"This castle used to be in England," Great-grandma Olive told us. "Lord Beardsly sent it to me in America stone by stone. It was a gift for catching the thief who stole his wife's emerald tiara."

Wow! I thought. Ashley and I have solved a lot of cases, but no one ever gave us a castle!

Being at Great-grandma Olive's detective headquarters was so great! It was Great-grandma Olive who made me and Ashley want to be detectives. She taught us everything we know. And she knows everything!

"Over to the right is our computer center,"

Great-grandma Olive told us. "All the detectives do their research here."

"How many detectives use the detective headquarters?" Ashley asked.

"Fifty-two," Great-grandma Olive replied. "That's why I like to think of the castle as more of a detective clubhouse. It's a place where so many detectives can talk over cases and share tips. Only there aren't many detectives here now because it's dinnertime."

A tall, skinny, bald man in a dark blue suit stepped out of the computer center. He marched over to us. "I still don't think it's fair, Olive!" he said. "Not fair at all!"

"What's not fair now, Zachary?" she replied.

"That we have to *share* the Detective of the Year award tomorrow night!" he answered.

Ashley grabbed my arm. "That's Zachary Ogden, one of the most famous detectives in America," she whispered. "The FBI called him for help on two cases last year!"

Great-grandma Olive flipped her braid over

her shoulder and sighed. "It's completely fair," she told Zachary. "You know the rules. The detective who solves the most cases wins the award. We tied this year. So we share it."

"But my last case was harder than your last case!" he announced.

"Zachary, you haven't met my great-grand-daughters," she said, changing the subject. "This is Mary-Kate and this is Ashley. They're ten years old and in the fifth grade. But this week they're on spring break. They're going to help me decorate the dining room for the Detective of the Year banquet."

Zachary looked totally bored.

"They're detectives, too," Great-grandma Olive added. "They run the Olsen and Olsen Mystery Agency out of the attic of their house in California."

"Oh, great," Zachary muttered. "Just what we need around here! Kid detectives hoping to get some tips!"

"Baloney!" a voice cried from behind us.

"Rotten baloney!" someone else added.

I spun around and saw Baby and Bobbi Butterworth. Ashley and I met the Butterworth twins last year at the old detective clubhouse.

Baby and Bobbi both had lots of short, curly red hair. And both women wore identical white sleeveless dresses. But Baby's shoes were hot pink, and Bobbi's were bright orange.

"You could probably pick up a tip or two—" Bobbi said to Zachary.

"From the Trenchcoat Twins," Baby finished. "They're famous, too!"

I grinned at Ashley. Baby and Bobbi were really nice!

Zachary rolled his eyes, then rushed back into the computer center.

"Time to start decorating the dining room for the banquet!" Great-grandma Olive said. "Mary-Kate and Ashley, the decorations are in a big red bag in the library. Will you go get it for me? First door at the top of the staircase."

"Sure," Ashley said. She led the way up the huge curving staircase.

She flung open the library door—and froze. I smashed right into her back.

"Why did you stop like that?" I asked. Ashley didn't answer. She just pointed into the library.

I peered over her shoulder—and gasped.

The room was a mess! The chairs, desks, and the sofa were all upside down. The suit of armor in the corner was upside down, too— and there was a cowboy hat on his feet! Books were flung all over the room!

"Who? What?" Ashley said.

"I don't know," I answered.

I heard a muffled ringing sound. I glanced around the room and spotted a phone lying upside down next to one of the upside-down desks. "Should we answer it?" I asked.

"I guess so," Ashley said.

We hurried over to the phone and I picked it up. "Hello. Detective headquarters," I said.

I heard someone laughing and laughing on the other end. I motioned Ashley closer so she could hear, too. "Who is this?" I asked.

The laughter got louder. The sound was totally creepy. I felt all the little hairs on the back of my neck stand up.

"Who is this?" I cried.

"Surprise!" a high, squeaky voice said. "Who am I and why did I destroy the library? That's for me to know—and for Olive Olsen to find out! And she'd better take this case—or else!"

THE SINGING DRAGON

"Or else what?" I yelled into the phone. "What are you talking about?"

The only answer was more laughter. The kind of freaky laughter a cartoon character would make.

Ashley leaned even closer. "Listen for any background sounds," she whispered. "They could be clues."

Click! The second Ashley said the word *clues*, the mystery caller hung up the phone.

Ashley took the receiver away from me and

hung it up. "I'll go get Great-grandma Olive and tell her what happened," she said.

A few minutes later I heard footsteps coming back up the stairs. Great-grandma Olive and Ashley hurried over to me.

Great-grandma Olive raised one eyebrow as she walked to the center of the room. She looked all around.

Great-grandma Olive always says a good detective has to stay calm and keep her eyes open. She says seeing all there is to see is the first step to solving a crime.

Great-grandma Olive studied the ceiling. She studied the floor. She turned around in a circle and studied each of the walls. "Hmmm," she said.

"Do you have any idea why the mystery caller said *you* have to take the case?" I asked her.

"No. At least not yet," she admitted. Great-grandma Olive turned in another slow circle. "Could you tell if the caller was a man or a

woman?" she asked.

"The voice was really high," I answered. "But it sounded fake. Like a cartoon voice."

"I think the caller might have used one of those toys that changes the way voices sound," Ashley said.

"Hmmm," Great-grandma Olive said one more time. Then she knelt down on the carpet. She pushed aside some books and pressed the top of her head against the floor.

She stretched her legs into the air and held herself in a perfect headstand. "On your heads, girls," she said. "Since lots of things in the room were turned upside-down, I think we should be upside down, too."

Great idea! I thought. I watched Ashley push herself into a perfect headstand. Her toes were perfectly straight and she didn't wobble or anything.

I squatted down next to her and pressed my head on the floor. I kicked my legs up—and flopped over onto my side.

I took a deep breath and tried again. I jiggled back and forth a lot, but I managed to stay balanced on my head.

"Hey!" Ashley cried. "Look at that!"

Ashley's voice surprised me. Ker-plop! I toppled to the floor again.

"Ashley, you made me fall," I complained.

Ashley sprang to her feet. She grabbed my hand and pulled me toward the bookshelves lining the far wall. "You have to see this," she called to Great-grandma Olive.

"Every book is turned upside down. Except for the ones in this row," Ashley said.

Great-grandma Olive hurried up behind us. "Good work, Ashley," she said.

"I wouldn't have seen it if you hadn't told us to stand on our heads," Ashley responded.

"Do you think the person who did this just missed a spot?" I asked.

"The right-side-up books are in the middle of the middle shelf," Ashley answered. "They would be hard to miss."

I nodded. That made sense to me.

"I just noticed something else that's strange," Great-grandma Olive said. "We keep the books in the library divided by subject. But this row has a animal book next to a cookbook next to a science book."

She walked down the row of shelves. "All the other books seem to be in the right places—just upside down," she told us.

"So whoever did this went out of his or her way to arrange this section of books," Ashley said. "But why?"

"I think this is a message from the person who did this," Great-grandma Olive said. "We just have to figure out how to read it."

I studied the right-side-up books. There were thin ones and fat ones. Tall ones and short ones. Hardcovers and paperbacks. But I didn't see any pattern in the way they were arranged.

Great-grandma Olive began to read the titles of the books. *"Tigers in the Wild. How to*

Cook Beans. Electricity and You. Doorknobs of the World."

She shook her head. "I thought maybe the words in the titles might form some kind of coded message. But they don't seem to."

I read the next few titles. *Royalty in the Ant Kingdom. Art and Architecture. Gone Fishing. Opera Stars. Nice Is Nice.*

Great-grandma Olive was right. The words in the titles didn't really go together.

"Maybe we should try rearranging the letters in the titles," Ashley suggested. She pulled her detective notebook and a pencil out of her pocket.

I decided to start with the letters in *Opera Stars.* I could make the words "tar" and "rat" and "tap" and "pat" and "stop" and "top" and "rap" and "sap" and "part" and "rasp" and "so."

"I couldn't find any message in the *Opera Stars* letters," I announced. "I'll try another book." I studied the books in the row. Which one should I work on next?

I felt a little tingle run from just under my ponytail all the way down my back. "Hey! The first letter of the titles of the first three books spells out *the*. T-H-E."

"Mary-Kate, I'll bet that's it!" Ashley exclaimed. "Just read the first letter of *each* book's title—that's probably the code!"

"T-H-E-D-R-A-G-O-N," Ashley spelled out. "That spells *the dragon*! You're brilliant, Mary-Kate!"

"Keep going!" Great-grandma Olive cried. "You're on to something now!"

Ashley slowly read the words formed by the first letter of each book's title. "The… dragon…sings…at…dawn."

"What is that supposed to mean?" I asked. "Dragons don't sing."

"What do you think, Great-grandma Olive?" Ashley asked.

"Right now I'm more worried about *who* left the message than what it means," Great-grandma Olive answered.

"Why?" I asked.

"During the day we keep the clubhouse unlocked," she said. "There are always so many detectives working here. We figured a stranger couldn't walk in without one of us noticing."

"That means the person who did this is someone everyone in the clubhouse knows!" Ashley exclaimed.

My heart gave a hard thump against my ribs. "That means all of the detectives are suspects!"

3

THE BET!

Great-grandma Olive hurried over to the intercom next to the door. She pushed down the little button and spoke into the speaker. "Will everyone please come to the library immediately," she said.

She turned to me and Ashley. "We shouldn't tell anyone we suspect one of the detectives. Not until we have proof."

Ashley and I both nodded. A few seconds later, I could hear people rushing up the stairs.

The first person through the door was

Great-grandma Olive's best friend, Henrietta Morgan. Henrietta's brown eyes were open really wide.

"Henrietta, I didn't expect to see you here today!" Great-grandma Olive exclaimed.

"I dropped by to give you some more vacation brochures," Henrietta explained. "I heard your announcement on my way in. What happened in here?"

Great-grandma Olive didn't have time to answer. Baby and Bobbi Butterworth burst into the library. They both began to scream.

Zachary Ogden arrived next.

Great-grandma Olive stuck her fingers in her mouth and gave a long, loud whistle. Everyone got very quiet very fast.

They listened hard as Great-grandma Olive told them about the weird phone call and the strange coded message.

"But I *can't* take the case," she said. "I'm very busy with another case. Plus, I was chosen to do the decorating for the banquet."

"I know why you don't want this case," Zachary snapped. "You know this mystery is too hard for you, Olive! You're afraid you *can't* solve it!"

"That's not true, Zachary," Great-grandma Olive said. "If I took the case, I could solve it right away—with a little investigating."

"Oh, really!" Zachary yelled. "Well, I'll bet you anything that you *can't* solve this mystery by the banquet tomorrow night. Even with the *famous* Trenchcoat Twins helping you!"

"I'll bet you that we can!" Great-grandma Olive replied.

"You're on!" Zachary exclaimed. "And here's what we'll bet: If you solve the mystery by tomorrow night, *you* win the Detective of the Year award by yourself. And if you *don't* solve it, *I* win the award."

Great-grandma Olive and Zachary shook hands. "The bet is on!" Zachary said with a huge smile. "You all heard it!" Then he rushed out of the library.

"Olive," Baby said. "Bobbi and I will be more than happy to—"

"Take over the decorating!" Bobbi finished. "We loved being in charge of the decorating last year. We really wanted to do it again this year, anyway."

"Oh, thank you...but no," Great-grandma Olive told them. "It's my responsibility."

Baby and Bobbi looked disappointed. "Okay, everyone," Great-grandma Olive said. "Go on back downstairs. My partners and I need to discuss the case."

I liked hearing Great-grandma Olive call Ashley and me her partners. It was going to be so cool working together! This was a dream come true for Ashley and me because Great-grandma Olive is an expert at investigating!

Everyone but Henrietta left the library.

She hurried over to Great-grandma Olive and shoved a stack of brochures into her hands. The top one had a picture of the Eiffel Tower in Paris on the front.

"We need to make plans for our vacation by the end of next week," Henrietta said.

"I promise I'll look at the brochures," Great-grandma Olive said. "And I promise this year we *will* go on vacation."

Henrietta laughed. "Your great-grandma says that every year," she told me and Ashley. "But we've never gone on vacation together. Not even once."

"I always have too many cases," Great-grandma Olive explained. "Every time I win the Detective of the Year award, my picture gets in all the newspapers. And then a lot of people want me to solve mysteries for them."

She smiled at Henrietta. "But this year we're taking our vacation. Really."

Henrietta nodded. "I hope so," she said. "Well, I'd better let you get started. See you later." She hurried out of the library.

Great-grandma Olive sat down on the top of the upside-down couch.

"So, what are your ideas for solving the

case?" I asked her. I couldn't wait to hear her expert investigation plan! She'd said she could solve the case in no time!

"I don't know!" Great-grandma Olive cried. "I don't have a clue!"

THE OLSEN AND OLSEN AND OLSEN TEAM

I stared at Great-grandma Olive. Was world-famous detective Olive Olsen saying she didn't know how to solve a case?

"I can't possibly solve this mystery by tomorrow night!" she said with a sigh. "I have to work on my other case—it's very important. I just won't have time to work on this one," she added sadly.

Ashley and I looked at each other.

"I can't believe I agreed to that stupid bet!" she told us. "But Zachary made me so angry!"

"Wait a minute!" I exclaimed. "You heard what Zachary said. That you wouldn't be able to solve the case *even with* our help!"

"That means *we* can solve the case for you," Ashley said. "So you can work on your other case!"

"Well…" Great-grandma Olive started to say.

"Don't worry!" I said. "You taught us everything we know about being detectives! We'll have this case solved by sundown tomorrow. And you'll win the Detective of the Year award yourself!"

"Okay, girls!" Great-grandma Olive said. "I know you two will do it!" She gave us each a kiss on the cheek, then left the room.

"So, how exactly will we have this case solved before the banquet tomorrow night?" Ashley asked me.

"I don't know," I said. "But we have to help Great-grandma Olive. If we don't solve the case, she'll lose the award!"

"Okay—let's plan where we should start

investigating," Ashley said.

"That coded message in the library," I said. "'The dragon sings at dawn'. We have to find out what that means."

"But how?" Ashley asked.

"I know!" I said. "By being in the library at dawn—to see if something happens!"

"That's a good idea," Ashley said. "We've done stakeouts before. We know what to look out for."

Right! I thought. But this time we were looking out for a singing dragon!

I clicked on my mini-tape recorder. Great-grandma Olive gave it to me when Ashley and I decided to become detectives.

"It is now seven forty-two p.m.," I said into the tiny speaker. "Ashley and I are in the library at the detective clubhouse. We're on an overnight stakeout. But only Great-grandma Olive knows that. Everyone else thinks we're here to clean up the library—even if it takes

all night!"

Click-clack. Click-clack. I heard high heels coming up the stairs. "One of the detectives must need a book from the library," I said to Ashley.

"Remember that all the detectives are suspects," Ashley whispered. "Keep an eye out for clues."

The library door swung open—and Baby and Bobbi pranced inside.

"We have some decorating ideas—" Bobbi began.

"For your great-grandma to look at," Baby finished.

"Great-grandma Olive won't be here until tomorrow morning. She had to do a stakeout for one of her other cases," Ashley explained.

"Oh, galoshes!" Bobby exclaimed.

"Muddy galoshes!" Baby cried. Their mouths curved down in identical frowns.

Baby handed Ashley a big envelope. "Would you show her these sketches for the dining

room decorations as soon as possible?" Baby asked. "If she—"

"Likes them, we want to get started right away," Bobbi said. "All she has to do is say yes—"

"And we'll do the rest," Baby concluded. "We know she's very busy with her big case and this one, too!" She and Bobbi smiled and left the library.

I heard footsteps coming up the stairs again. A second later, Henrietta hurried into the library. "I brought you a snack," she told us. She handed Ashley a bag of fresh-baked chocolate-chip cookies.

"I have to run," Henrietta said. "I'll lock up on my way out—I have Olive's extra keys. You two are the only ones left in the clubhouse."

"Thanks," Ashley and I said together.

"Oh, and will you give Olive these for me?" Henrietta reached into her bag and pulled out more vacation brochures. "Remind her that we have to make our reservations soon if we're

going to go on vacation next month."

"We'll make her look at them," Ashley promised.

"We'll sit on her if we have to," I added.

Henrietta gave us a little wave and rushed off.

"She's nice," I said.

"Yeah," Ashley agreed. "I can hardly believe she and Great-grandma Olive have been friends since they were ten—our age."

I ate one of the cookies. "I need something to do to keep me awake all night," I said. "I think I'm going to turn all the books right-side up."

"Good idea," Ashley answered. "We already dusted for fingerprints and checked for any other coded messages. There's no reason not to start cleaning up since we didn't find anything."

It took hours and hours to get the books back in order. I checked my watch when I slid the last book in place. It was almost midnight.

Midnight. There was something a little spooky about being in the big old castle that late at night. All alone.

Ashley pulled her detective notebook out of her back pocket.

"Why do you think the caller wanted Great-grandma Olive to solve the mystery?" Ashley asked.

"I don't know," I said. "But I think it's a clue. A weird clue."

Ashley nodded. "Let's make a list of the detectives who were in the clubhouse when we found the library messed up," she suggested.

"Okay, there were Baby and Bobbi," I said. "And Zachary."

"Let's ask Great-grandma Olive for a list of *all* the detectives' names tomorrow morning," Ashley said. "They're *all* suspects."

I pressed my fingers against her lips. "I think I heard something downstairs," I whispered.

"But we're the only ones in the clubhouse,"

Ashley whispered back.

We both listened hard.

THUD! THUD!

Ashley grabbed my arm. "What *is* that?" she asked.

"I don't know," I said. "All I know is we are definitely *not* alone in here."

5

THE GIANT FLYING BUNNY!

*T*hud. *Thud. Thud.*

"We have to get downstairs," Ashley said. "We might be able to solve this mystery right now!"

She jumped to her feet and raced to the library door. I was right behind her.

Thud. Thud. Thud.

I followed Ashley out into the hall. It was really dark! "Ashley, I'll get our flashlights. Wait here!" I ran back into the library, pulled our flashlights out of our backpacks, and

raced out the door.

We switched on our flashlights. Then we tiptoed over to the staircase and started down.

Ashley paused at the bottom of the stairs. "Which way should we go?" she whispered.

I listened for the next *thud*. But the huge castle was silent.

But that didn't mean whoever made the noises wasn't still inside. Watching us.

"I guess we should just start checking rooms," I whispered.

"I'll go left. You go right," Ashley said.

I nodded. I crept down the hall to the first door. I pressed my ear against it. I didn't hear anything.

I opened it a crack and peered inside. Empty. Totally empty. There wasn't even any furniture.

One door down. About a million to go, I thought. The clubhouse is huge!

I inched my way over to the next door. My back felt itchy. I couldn't stop imagining that

someone was watching every move I made.

I took a deep breath and reached for the doorknob.

"Mary-Kate!" Ashley shouted. "Come quick!"

I spun around and raced toward the sound of Ashley's voice. My heart was pounding like crazy against my ribs. "Where are you?" I yelled.

"Dining room," she called back.

I raced down the hall and burst into the room. I saw Ashley staring at black footprints on the floor.

Enormous footprints.

Each one was bigger than my head!

I did a quick check of the room. I wanted to make sure that whatever made the footprints wasn't still around.

"What could have made these?" Ashley asked.

"Some kind of animal," I answered. "A *giant* animal!"

I bent down to get a closer look. Each paw print was divided into round sections. Sort of like the pads on the bottom of a dog's foot. But these prints were more oval-shaped.

I stood up and followed the trail of paw prints across the floor.

"Um, Ashley," I gulped. "Look where the paw prints go!"

Ashley's glance followed the paw prints as they continued up the wall—and straight across the ceiling!

"This doesn't make any sense!" I said. "What kind of animal can walk on the ceiling?"

"I don't know," Ashley said. "But I'll bet there's a book on animal tracks in the library. I'll go upstairs and look. I'll be right back."

"Be careful," I said. "Whatever made these tracks might still be in the clubhouse."

Ashley came back a few minutes later with a book. We flipped through the pages, looking back and forth from the drawings in the book to the huge tracks.

"The paw prints are as big as elephant tracks," Ashley said. "But they don't look like elephant tracks at all."

"Keep going," I said. "Remember that the tracks have to be made by something that can walk across a ceiling."

"They don't match tiger tracks, either," Ashley said. "Or wolf tracks. Or any kind of bird tracks. And they don't match gorilla tracks. Or deer tracks. Or armadillo tracks."

Ashley turned another page in the book.

"That's it!" I exclaimed, staring at the page. "That's a match."

"But it can't be," Ashley said, frowning. She studied the page.

"Why?" I asked. "What kind of animal is that?"

"It's a bunny!" she said.

A bunny? I thought. How could a bunny have made these giant paw prints? Or walked up the wall and across the ceiling?

"The only bunny that could have made

these tracks is a *giant* bunny." I shook my head, confused.

"Yeah," Ashley answered. She glanced at the paw prints on the ceiling. "A giant *flying* bunny!"

Singing dragons and giant flying bunnies! The clues in this case made no sense.

The phone rang. Ashley and I stared at each other.

"Do you think that's our mystery caller?" I asked her.

"Let's find out!" she said. We ran into the hallway and picked up the phone.

"Detective headquarters," I said, holding my breath. Ashley leaned in close so she could listen.

The caller didn't say anything. "Hello?" I said again. "Hello? Who is this?"

"That's the surprise!" the high, squeaky voice answered.

Then the phone went dead.

THE COUNTDOWN BEGINS!

I hung up the phone. "The surprise will be on the caller when we figure out who it is!" I announced.

"Yeah!" Ashley said. "Let's take a closer look at those paw prints. Maybe there's a clue somewhere."

We headed back to the dining room. That's when we noticed there were some faint paw prints on the hallway walls, too. In the dining room, I bent down really close to the paw prints. I brushed my finger across one of

them—I never touched a giant flying bunny's paw print before!

"Ashley, it's wet!" I said. I stared at my finger—there was a smudge on the tip!

Ashley bent down and leaned really close to the paw prints. She sniffed it. "It's paint!" she said. "Someone painted these on!"

"Weird!" I said, frowning.

"Really weird," Ashley agreed.

"Let's wash these prints off the walls and ceiling," I said. "Great-grandma Olive has to decorate in here tomorrow morning."

"Yeah," Ashley said. "Then we can go back to the library and try to get some sleep. We'll set our alarm clock for dawn—and see if that singing dragon code did mean something."

We nodded, and we got to work. By the time we got back to the library, we were both really tired. We each curled up on one of the sofas.

"Mary-Kate," Ashley said. "We have to solve this case by tomorrow night. We told Great-

grandma Olive we could do it."

"I know," I said. "But we have all day tomorrow."

"That's true," Ashley said. "We'll figure out what these strange clues mean—and solve the case by sundown."

We had to. Or it would be our fault that Great-grandma Olive didn't win the Detective of the Year award!

"Should we tell Great-grandma Olive that nothing happened at dawn?" I asked Ashley the next morning.

"I don't think so," she replied as we headed downstairs. "I don't think we should tell her about the bunny tracks, either. Or that we got another weird phone call."

"Why?" I asked. "We could use her help!"

"I know," Ashley said, "but she might worry that we're no closer to solving the case than we were yesterday!"

Ashley is right, I thought. We can't let

Great-grandma Olive know how worried we are. She has her own case to think about.

We found Great-grandma Olive in the dining room. She was spreading a huge tablecloth on the long, wood table. It was decorated with tiny magnifying glasses.

I looked around the room. No one would ever suspect there were giant bunny paw prints all over this room last night.

"Henrietta left some brochures for you to check out," Ashley told Great-grandma Olive.

"Ashley and I promised we'd make you look at them," I said.

"I must do that," Great-grandma Olive said. "Henrietta will be so disappointed if we don't go on our vacation."

"Baby and Bobbi came over last night, too," Ashley added. "They dropped off some decorating sketches for you to look at."

Great-grandma Olive shook her head. "I know they're just trying to be nice. But everyone thought they did a terrible job on last

year's decorations. I wouldn't want them ever to know that, but I can't let them do it again!"

"Have you three detectives solved the big mystery in the library yet?" a loud voice asked. Zachary Ogden marched into the dining room.

"You know a good detective doesn't discuss his or her cases with anyone, Zachary," Great-grandma Olive said. She winked at me and Ashley.

I smiled. That was one of the first things Great-grandma Olive taught us about being detectives.

"I'm looking forward to having that award all to myself!" Zachary said with a sneaky smile.

"You're here awfully early, Zachary," Great-grandma Olive commented.

"I'm doing some research on the computer," he said, then left the room.

We helped Great-grandma Olive hang the Detective of the Year award banner on the wall. Then we taped cardboard magnifying

glasses all over the room.

After we finished decorating, we looked around the dining room.

"Looks great, girls!" Great-grandma Olive said. "Thanks for all your help."

"No problem," I said. "Maybe you could help us with something."

"Sure, what is it?" she asked.

"Do you have a list of all the detectives who use the clubhouse?" I asked.

"Yes," she said. "I'll print out a copy of our member list for you. It has their names, addresses, and phone numbers."

"Great!" Ashley said. "We need it for our investigation."

"Just let me go freshen up first. I'm off to interview a suspect in my big case. I'll get you that list before I go."

We watched Great-grandma Olive leave the room. She looked calm. As if she had faith that we would solve the case.

"Okay," I said to Ashley. "We need to figure

out the motive. Maybe that will help us narrow down our suspects."

Motive is one of the words Great-grandma Olive taught us. It means a person's reason for doing something.

"Right," Ashley responded. "Why would one of the detectives destroy the *detective* clubhouse?"

"Maybe one of the detectives is trying to stop the banquet," I said. "Maybe that person thinks he or she should win the award—not Great-grandma Olive *or* Zachary."

Ashley nodded. "That would be a good motive for someone wrecking the dining room," she said. "This is where the banquet is going to be held. But what about messing up the library? That wouldn't stop the banquet."

"True," I said, thinking hard. "Do you think—" I began.

But I was interrupted by a scream. A long, shrill scream.

"That was Great-grandma Olive!" I yelled.

DETECTIVE TRICK

ANIMAL TRACKING

Did you or a friend lose a pet? Finding a lost animal can be easy. Follow its tracks—and you just might find that missing cat sleeping in a tree. Or the disappearing puppy digging up your neighbor's yard. Or the lost bunny rabbit hopping under the bushes.

Dog:

Rabbit:

Cat:

If you have a different pet, make a sketch of its footprints. Then you'll have its footprints on file!

The Case Of The SURPRISE CALL

DETECTIVE TRICK

BACKWARDS WORD CODE

No one but you and your friend will be able to read your private notes—if you use our cool backwards word code! Just write each sentence backwards, like this:

!Nuf dna looc si evitceted a gnieb

This sentence in the backwards word code says:

Being a detective is cool and fun!

Look for our next mystery…
The Case Of The DISAPPEARING PRINCESS

CRAZY CLUES!

Ashley and I raced toward the bathroom. We burst through the open door.

"What's wrong?" Ashley cried.

"I'm sorry I scared you," Great-grandma Olive said. She sounded like her usual calm self. "Just take a look in the sink—and try not to scream like I did!"

I peered into the sink. It was filled with thick purple goo.

"What is that?" Ashley squealed. Her nose was all wrinkled up—like she smelled some-

thing rotten.

But nothing smelled rotten in the bathroom. Something smelled...sweet. Like grapes.

No, not grapes.

"It's Jell-O!" I exclaimed. "It's just grape Jell-O!" I pointed to the empty box in the trash basket.

"I wish I could stay and deal with this," Great-grandma Olive said. "But I'm already running late. I'll go get that list you need." She hurried away, then came back with two sheets of paper.

"Here you go," she said, handing Ashley the list. "I'd better run—I'll see you later."

Ashley folded up the list and put it in her pocket. Then she pulled out her detective notebook. She added "Jell-O in sink" under the CLUES heading.

"You think the Jell-O is definitely part of our case?" I asked.

"Our suspect has been wrecking the club-

house room by room," Ashley said. "Jell-O in the sink seems to go with painted bunny paw prints in the dining room and all the weird stuff that was done to the library."

"Let's make a list of everyone who is in the clubhouse right now," I suggested. "We need to know who could have slipped in here and made the Jell-O."

"Whoever we're after could have done this last night," Ashley answered. "We haven't been in this bathroom since we found the paw prints at midnight."

"You're right," I said. "There's no reason to think the person who did this is in the club-house right now. So what do—" I began.

I stopped talking. I noticed Baby and Bobbi standing in the doorway, listening to us. Their eyes were locked on the sink.

"Wow!" Bobbi exclaimed.

"Double wow!" Baby said. "Bunny paw-prints in the dining room—"

"And now Jell-O in the sink," Bobbi added.

"We're sorry for listening in, but—"

"We didn't want to interrupt your case discussion," Baby finished.

"We saw your great-grandmother on her way out," Bobbi said.

"She told us she liked our decorating sketches," Baby added.

"But that she had the decorating all under control," Bobbi announced.

"It's too bad," Baby said with a sigh. "We really wanted—"

"To be in charge of decorating again this year," Bobbi finished. "Oh, well!"

"We'd better get home," Baby said. We're working—"

"On a really big case!" Bobbi exclaimed. They smiled at us and then left.

Ashley and I went into the library to discuss our case in private. We didn't want anyone to overhear us. All of the detectives were possible suspects.

"Okay—back to figuring out a motive,"

Ashley said. "Why would someone destroy the library? Leave a code about a singing dragon? Paint bunny paw prints in the dining room? Make Jell-O in the sink? Call and say that Great-grandma Olive had to take the case?"

"I don't know," I said.

"Me, either," Ashley responded.

"Maybe we should try to figure out what all those things have in common," I suggested.

"Great idea!" Ashley said. "That might tell us something about the clues!"

We both thought hard. "Nothing." I said. "Those things have absolutely nothing in common that I can think of."

"Yeah," Ashley agreed. "Nothing."

"Wait a minute!" I exclaimed, jumping up from the sofa. "That's it! Those things have *nothing* in common!"

"I know. We just agreed to that," Ashley said.

"But that's the big clue!" I said. "The clues have *nothing* in common!"

"But what does that mean?" Ashley asked, frowning.

"It means that someone is trying very hard to confuse us!" I exclaimed.

"Mary-Kate, that's it!" Ashley cried.

"That's what?" I asked, confused.

"You just figured out the motive!" Ashley exclaimed. "And I just figured out who suspect #1 is!"

8

PURPLE GOO=SUSPECT #1

"**Z**achary Ogden is our first suspect!" Ashley announced.

"I don't get it," I said. "What motive does Zachary have?"

"He's trying to confuse us! That's all. That's his motive," Ashley explained.

"Right!" I cried. "Because he wants the Detective of the Year award all to himself. He destroyed the library. Then he called and demanded Great-grandma Olive take the case. And then he had the perfect excuse to make

that bet with her."

"So Zachary created a case that makes no sense at all," Ashley said. "A case he's sure we'll never solve. That way, Great-grandma Olive will lose the bet!"

Ashley flipped open her notebook. "It makes sense," she said. "But we need proof."

I jumped up and headed for the door.

"Where are you going?" Ashley asked.

"I have a plan," I said. "But to make it work, I need to get some of that purple Jell-O from the sink!"

About an hour later, Ashley and I stood on Zachary's front porch. He lived just a few blocks away from detective headquarters.

"Remember to watch Zachary's face when I show him the Jell-O," I told Ashley.

That was my plan. I wanted to observe Zachary's reaction when he saw the Jell-O. I hoped he *might* do something to give himself away.

"I'll remember," Ashley promised. "But you have to remember that even if he looks really guilty, it isn't real proof."

"I know, I know," I answered. "This is just a place to start our investigation."

I stuck the jar of Jell-O behind my back. Then I rang Zachary's doorbell.

Zachary swung open the door. He raised his eyebrows when he saw me and Ashley. "It's the junior detectives," he said.

"We need your help," Ashley said. "We have a sample of some kind of *goo*. We thought you might be able to tell us what it is."

"Everyone at detective headquarters told us how smart you are," I added.

Zachary's chest puffed way out. "Come on in," he said. "I'd be happy to give you my expert opinion."

Zachary led the way into the living room. Ashley and I sat down on the couch.

"Let me see the—" Zachary began.

A ringing telephone interrupted him.

"Be right back," he said. He hurried out of the room.

"Look over there!" Ashley whispered. She jerked her chin toward a framed photograph on top of the TV.

I leaned forward and studied it. It was of two people dressed up as bunnies.

Bunnies! I checked out their feet.

"Those feet look about the right size to make the tracks we found," I whispered back.

"Nice picture, isn't it?" Zachary asked.

I gave a little squeak. I didn't hear him come back in the room!

"Really nice," Ashley said.

"That was taken at the detective club's last Halloween party," Zachary told us. "I was sure I was going to win the trophy for best costume."

His voice got louder. "But then some fool showed up in the *same* costume—and we tied for first place. I know I got mine first. It wasn't fair," he bellowed.

"Uh, who was in the other bunny costume?" I asked.

"I don't remember who that was," he muttered. "Why don't you show me that goo."

"Here it is." I slowly pulled the jar of Jell-O out from behind my back.

I stared at Zachary. I was afraid to blink. I didn't want to miss the expression on his face when he realized the goo was grape Jell-O.

Zachary unscrewed the jar. He brought it to his nose and took a tiny sniff.

"Smells like grape jam!" he said. He took a little spoonful of the Jell-O and tasted it. "Just as I thought, it's—"

Zachary didn't finish his sentence. "Excuse me for a moment," he mumbled. "I'll be right back." He thrust the Jell-O back at me. Then he rushed out of the room.

I turned to Ashley. "Did you see that? He knows we're on to him! *And* he has a bunny suit! He's our bad guy!"

9

CAUGHT YOU!

"**D**on't start jumping to conclusions, Mary-Kate," Ashley warned. "We need proof before we—"

She stopped in mid-sentence. Zachary hurried back into the room with a washcloth pressed against his forehead.

There were bright red splotches all over his face and neck.

He sank down in the big brown chair next to the couch. "I can tell you what that goo is, girls. I thought it was grape jelly, but it's not.

It's grape Jell-O!" he said. "I'm terribly, terribly allergic to it."

Uh-oh! "Do you need us to call a doctor?" I asked. I felt terrible!

Zachary lightly patted his face with the cloth. "No, I'll be fine," he said. "I just want to go lie down for a while."

"Okay," Ashley said. "We're sorry about the Jell-O."

"Really sorry," I added.

"There's no way you could have known," Zachary answered. "At least I was able to tell you what your goo is."

"Yeah," I said. "Thanks."

"Thanks," Ashley repeated. We hurried out the door.

"Well, we're back to zero suspects," I said.

"Maybe," Ashley said. "I doubt someone who's allergic to grape Jell-O would ever eat it knowingly. But he might have done it just to throw us off!"

"That's true," I said. "Let's not cross him off

our list just yet."

"We do have a great new clue," Ashley said. "The bunny costume from that photo in Zachary's house."

"We have to find out which detective was in the *other* bunny costume," I said. "I'm sure he or she used the big bunny feet to make the paw prints!"

Ashley pulled the list of the detectives' names and addresses out of her pocket.

"We have a lot of people to talk to," she said, looking at the list. "There are fifty-two names here!"

"What's the first name on the list?" I asked.

"Baby Butterworth," Ashley answered.

"I can think of a motive for her and Bobbi!" I exclaimed. "They really, really wanted to do the decorating for the banquet. But Great-grandma Olive was chosen this year."

"You're brilliant, Mary-Kate!" Ashley said. She gave me a high five. "Baby and Bobbi probably wanted to give Great-grandma Olive

an impossible case. That way she would be too busy to do the decorating."

"Yeah. But Great-grandma Olive kept saying she could handle the decorating, so they had to make the case harder and harder!" I said.

"Plus Baby and Bobbi have been at the clubhouse every time something strange happened," Ashley reminded me.

Ashley gave a little bounce on her toes. "Next stop—Baby and Bobbi's!" she cried.

"This is it—24 Maple Drive," Ashley said.

The two-story house was painted pink, with orange trim. It almost hurt my eyes to look at the house—but I liked the colors.

Ashley and I hurried up the front walk. Pink and orange polka dots were painted on it all the way to the door.

I reached out and rang the doorbell. It made a funny sound—like a bird chirping.

No one answered.

"I guess they aren't home," Ashley said. We

started back down the walk.

"That code you came up with was so clever," I heard someone say. I recognized the voice. It was Baby talking.

I grabbed Ashley by the arm. I put my finger on my lips to signal we had to be very quiet.

Then I led the way over to the bright red gate at the side of the house.

I peeked through a crack in the gate. I could see Baby and Bobbi standing in the backyard.

"No, no. Those bunny paw prints you painted—*that* was clever," Bobbi said.

I pulled my mini-tape recorder out of my pocket. I clicked it on.

In one minute we would have the evidence we needed to close the case.

"You know what was really clever?" Baby asked. "The way we mixed up that batch of Jell-O in the sink!"

I grinned at Ashley. She gave me the

thumbs up.

Then the back gate swung open—and Baby and Bobbi pranced out.

"Oh, no!" Baby and Bobbi cried at the same time when they saw us.

"The Trenchcoat Twins—" Baby said.

"Caught us!" Bobbi finished.

10

WHO'S THAT BUNNY?

"**W**e got it all on tape!" I shouted, holding up my mini-tape recorder. "Case closed!"

"You think—" Baby exclaimed.

"That *we* did all the horrible things at the detective clubhouse," Bobbi finished. "But we didn't."

Ashley planted her hands on her hips. "We *heard* you say you painted the bunny paw prints. We *heard* you say you made the Jell-O."

"No, no! You just caught us trying to—" Baby began.

"Solve the case," Bobbi continued. "Your great-grandma told us that it helps to pretend—"

"That you are the suspect you are looking for," Baby picked up where her sister left off.

Ashley's eyes narrowed as she studied Baby and Bobbi. "But it's not your case," she reminded them. "Why would you be trying to solve it?"

Good question, I thought. Ashley is so logical. That's one of the things that makes her a great partner.

"We wanted to help your great-grandma because—" Bobbi began to explain.

"We want her to win the award!" Baby said. "She's a great detective *and* a great person, but—"

"But Zachary is *just* a great detective," Bobbi finished. "He's not willing to help out club members the way your great-grandma does."

Ashley and I had to smile at that. But I still

didn't know what to think.

Baby and Bobbi *sounded* as if they were telling the truth.

And Great-grandma Olive *did* have a lot of interesting ways of working on a case. Maybe she did give them the idea of acting like the suspect they were looking for.

"Maybe you could help us out with some-thing," Ashley said. "We saw a picture in Zachary Ogden's house. It was of two people in bunny costumes at the detective club Halloween party. We know Zachary was one of the people. Do you know who the other one was?"

"Whoever it was tied with Zachary for best costume," Baby said.

"And *we* should have won," Bobbi added. "We *made* our costumes. We were strawberry ice-cream cones. The bunny costumes were store bought."

"But do you know who was wearing it?" I asked.

Baby and Bobbi both shrugged.

"We're sorry—" Bobbi said.

"But we just can't remember," Baby added.

"How about the store?" I asked. "Can you remember what store the costumes came from?"

"The Darling—" Baby said.

"Dress-up Shop," Bobbi concluded.

"Welcome to the Darling Dress-up Shop," a short, blond woman said. "I'm Tina Hodges, the owner. What can I do for you?"

"We're trying to track down two people who bought bunny costumes from you last Halloween," I answered.

"I should still have the sales receipts," Tina said. "I save everything." She reached under the counter and pulled out a thick black binder.

"Halloween, Halloween," she mumbled. She flipped through the mass of papers stuffed into the binder. "Found Halloween," Tina said.

"Now I just have to find bunny. Bunny, bunny, bunny."

If Tina could tell us who bought the second bunny outfit, our case would be practically closed. And Zachary could forget about hogging the Detective of the Year award.

"Got it," Tina said. "I sold five bunny costumes last Halloween. I have the receipts for all of them right here."

"Were all five costumes adult size?" Ashley asked.

Tina checked the receipts. "Nope. Only two. One was sold to Zachary Ogden. I remember that because he returned his the day after Halloween. Of all the nerve!"

I looked at Ashley. If Zachary *returned* his costume, that meant he couldn't have made those bunny tracks. We had to rule him out now!

And that meant the other person was definitely who we were after!

"Do you know who the other person was?"

Ashley asked.

"Let's see…" Tina said, flipping through the receipts.

I felt like grabbing the receipts out of Tina's hands. I had to know the other name! But I forced myself to stay still.

Tina shook her head. "Sorry. The top of the receipt—the part with the name—got torn off."

"Oh, no!" I exclaimed. What were we going to do?

Time was running out. The banquet was just two hours away!

I picked up the receipt and studied it. "I know how we can find out who this belongs to," I said.

"How?" Ashley asked.

"We could just go to this address," I replied, pointing to the receipt.

"It's dangerous," Ashley said.

"Yeah. But it's fast," I argued. "And we need fast. Or we'll never solve this case in time!"

11

MYSTERY HOUSE!

"**H**ere we are," I said, staring at the small brick house. I double-checked the address on the receipt.

Yes, this nice-looking house with all the flowers in the front yard was definitely the right one.

Ashley didn't move toward the house. Neither did I.

"Okay—I'll knock on the door," I said. "And when we see who answers, we'll make up some kind of story about why we're here. We

have to try to get inside."

Ashley nodded. "Yeah. We have to find the bunny suit and check the feet. If they have paint on the bottom—case closed."

I took a deep breath and headed across the lawn to the house. Ashley followed right behind me.

The door was slightly ajar. I knocked on the door. There was no answer. I knocked harder—really hard.

And the door swung open!

I put one foot inside.

"Mary-Kate, I'm not sure this is such a great idea," Ashley said.

I wasn't sure it was such a great idea, either. But time was running out.

"Hello," I called. "Is anyone home?"

No answer.

"We'll just take a fast peek in this closet right here," I said to Ashley. I gestured to a closet right by the door. The bunny suit might be in there!

I started to take another step inside. Ashley grabbed the back of my shirt and pulled me to a stop.

"We have to do this," I protested. "The banquet is only an hour and a half away!"

"That's not why I stopped you," she answered. "Look at that photo!" She pointed to a framed photograph on the foyer wall— two people in bunny suits.

"Well, at least we know this is the right house for sure," I said, staring at the photo.

Then I noticed something weird about the photo. The background looked the same—but the bunnies were sitting down in this photo, holding first-prize ribbons. In the one at Zach's, the bunnies were standing up.

I leaned over really close to study the picture. "Ashley! The bunny on the right has some long, dark hair flowing out of the bunny head!"

"Which detectives have long, dark hair?" Ashley asked.

"Let's see," I said, thinking. "Great-grandma

Olive has long *gray* hair. Zach has *no* hair. Baby and Bobbi have bright *red* hair, and there are a whole bunch of detectives we haven't met yet..."

"We can ask Great-grandma Olive which detectives have long, dark hair," Ashley said. "She's probably at the clubhouse making sure the decorations are perfect."

"Right!" I said. "Let's find that bunny suit. And then let's find Great-grandma Olive!

"Yeah," Ashley agreed. "Once we have the proof and know which detective we're looking for, we can confront him or her at the clubhouse. Before the banquet begins!"

I marched over to the hall closet and pulled open the door. The closet was huge.

I checked inside. There were a lot of coats hung on a rod. And behind that rod was another one, jammed with clothes.

I stepped farther into the closet. It was really dark—I couldn't see very well.

I pushed aside something cool and silky. I

felt something thick and scratchy. I felt something soft and velvety.

Then I felt something…furry.

I ran my fingers up the furry thing. It seemed to have a head with two ears. Two long, long ears.

"I found it!" I cried.

"Yes!" Ashley exclaimed. "We need to get the feet," she said. "If there is paint on the bottom, we'll have all the proof we need!"

I felt around the floor for the furry feet. "Where are they?" I mumbled.

"I'll help you look," Ashley called. She stepped into the closet.

Click!

"What was that?" I cried.

"The door shut behind me," Ashley said.

We ran over to the door. There was no knob on the inside!

I pushed the door—but it didn't budge.

"We're trapped!" I yelled.

THE MOTIVE

"**W**hat are we going to do?" I asked Ashley. "The banquet is just an hour away. We can't stay trapped in here—or Zachary will get the award!"

"We'd better think of something--fast!"

I thought hard. Aside from breaking down the door, I didn't know what to do. And I didn't think Ashley and I could break down the door even if we tried!

Click!

It sounded as if the front door opened.

"Should we scream?" I asked Ashley.

"It's our only way out," she replied. "We have to get out of here so we can win the award for Great-grandma Olive!"

"Help!" I screamed.

Ashley screamed, too.

I heard a click—then the closet door opened.

Great-grandma Olive stood there with her mouth hanging open.

"I expected to find a scarf in here to borrow for the banquet," Great-grandma Olive said to us. "Not my great-granddaughters! What are you doing in Henrietta's closet?"

Henrietta's closet? Ashley and I looked at each other. Both of our mouths were wide open.

"This is Henrietta's house?" I asked.

"Yes," Great-grandma Olive said. "Don't you know whose closet you're in?"

Ashley and I shook our heads.

"I don't understand," Great-grandma Olive

said. "But let's start with *why* you were in Henrietta's closet."

"We were looking for this," I said, holding up the bunny costume. "The final evidence we needed to prove who did those things to the clubhouse."

Ashley and I stepped out of the closet. We told Great-grandma Olive all about the bunny tracks in the dining room, our investigation, and how we ended up in Henrietta's closet.

"I can't believe it," Great-grandma Olive whispered.

"I'm sorry. I'm so sorry," a voice said from behind us.

Ashley, Great-grandma Olive, and I all spun around. Henrietta stood in the doorway to the house. Tears glistened in her eyes.

"I don't understand," Great-grandma Olive said.

"It was horrible and selfish of me," Henrietta answered. "But I...I didn't want you to win the Detective of the Year award. Not

this year."

I didn't get it. Henrietta was Great-grandma Olive's best friend. Why wouldn't she want Great-grandma Olive to win the award?

"Oh, I get it!" Ashley said. "If Great-grandma Olive won the award, she would get her picture in the newspapers. And then she'd get lots of new cases."

"Right!" I said, finally understanding. I turned to Henrietta. "And then she wouldn't be able to go on vacation with you."

"Is this true, Henrietta?" Great-grandma Olive asked.

Henrietta sniffled and nodded. Great-grandma Olive handed her a tissue.

"You destroyed the library to give Great-grandma Olive a case she couldn't solve," I said. "But how did you know Zachary would make the bet?"

"I didn't know," Henrietta said. She turned to Great-grandma Olive. "I decided to give you an unsolvable case. I figured you wouldn't

accept the award if you had a case you could-n't solve. Then Zachary jumped in and made that bet with you. He helped me with my plan without even realizing it."

Henrietta sniffled again. "I really didn't want to do anything bad to your great-grand-mother and especially not to the two of you," she explained to me and Ashley. "I just wanted somebody else to win the award."

She turned to Great-grandma Olive. "I was sure you would win again next year."

Henrietta wiped her eyes. "It was so silly of me to think there was a case you couldn't solve—especially with the help of the Trenchcoat Twins," she said. "I owe all three of you a huge apology."

Great-grandma Olive squeezed Henrietta's hand and smiled.

"Henrietta, why were you at the detective club's Halloween party, anyway?" I asked. "You're not a detective. That's why we didn't consider you a suspect"

"I cook all the food and bake all the desserts for the party," she explained. "So the detectives always invite me to dress up in a costume and enjoy myself."

"Now, *that* makes sense," I said. "You make the best chocolate-chip cookies in the world!"

Great-grandma Olive laughed.

I looked at my watch. "Oh, no!" I said. "We'd better get to the clubhouse and tell everyone the case is solved! The banquet starts in ten minutes!"

AND THE AWARD GOES TO...

13

"**G**ood evening, fellow detectives," a woman said from the head of the table at the banquet. "As you know, I'm Tracy Richman, this year's banquet planner."

Everyone clapped, then got really quiet. "As you also know," Tracy continued, "this year Olive Olsen and Zachary Ogden were to share the Detective of the Year award.

"But Olive and Zach made a bet. And therefore, I'm pleased to announce that the winner of this year's Detective of the Year award is—"

Everyone stared at Tracy Richman, waiting to hear who won the bet.

"Olive Olsen!" Tracy called out. "She solved the case of the clubhouse mystery before the banquet began. She wins the award!"

Baby and Bobbi gave squeals of delight. Henrietta let out a loud *hooray*.

But no one cheered harder than Ashley and I did.

Great-grandma Olive walked to the podium at the head of the table. Tracy handed her a big gold trophy.

"Being named Detective of the Year is a great honor," Great-grandma Olive said. "But I didn't solve the mystery at the clubhouse. I don't deserve the award."

"You heard her!" Zachary cried, jumping up from his seat. He rushed up to the podium and grabbed the trophy out of Great-grandma Olive's hand.

"I'm the *only* Detective of the Year this year!" he exclaimed, holding the trophy high

above his head.

Great-grandma Olive marched over to Zachary and took the award out of his hand. Then she walked straight over to me and Ashley. She set her big gold trophy down in front of us.

"As I was saying," she announced. "*I* didn't solve the case— my great-granddaughters did! They deserve the award!"

"But they're just kids!" Zachary yelled. "They're too young to be the Detectives of the Year! It's not fair!"

"Oh, pumpkin seeds!" Bobbi called out.

"Slimy pumpkin seeds!" Baby said. "The Trenchcoat Twins solved the case—"

"So they win the award!" Bobbi finished. "A bet is a bet!"

"You two are the real detectives of the year," Great-grandma Olive said to me and Ashley.

Ashley grinned at me. "Congratulations, Detective Olsen," she said.

"Congratulations, Detective Olsen," I answered.

Everyone clapped. Except Zachary. He was sulking!

Great-grandma Olive put her fingers in her mouth and gave a loud whistle. Everyone got quiet.

"Will you two handle the new case I got yesterday?" she said to Ashley and me. "I'm going on vacation with my very best friend."

The hugest smile I've ever seen broke across Henrietta's face.

Great-grandma Olive gave me and Ashley a big hug. "Enjoy your trophy," she said. "You did a great job with the case."

"Being great detectives—" Ashley began.

"Runs in the family!" I finished.

And the Trenchcoat Twins solved another case!

Hi from the both of us,

Ashley and I were in Hollywood! We won tickets to a movie premiere. That meant we were going to be the very first kids to see the hot new movie — "The Disappearing Princess." All our favorite movie stars were there. It was so exciting!

The movie was about a real Russian princess named Anna who disappeared. Talk about a mystery. But then another mystery unfolded right before our eyes!

You see, Princess Anna's favorite doll was on display in the theater lobby. But when the movie started, the doll disappeared!

We were asked to find it. And that's when things got really mysterious!

Want to find out more? Take a look at the sneak peek on the next page for The *New* Adventures of Mary-Kate & Ashley: The Case of The Disappearing Princess.

See you next time!

Love,

Ashley Olsen + Mary-Kate Olsen

A sneak peek at our next mystery…

The Case Of The
DISAPPEARING PRINCESS

"The Princess Anna doll is gone!" I screamed. I ran over to the doll's display case.

"*What?!*" I heard a woman shriek. It was Ruska, the woman in charge of the doll. She raced over to me and Ashley.

She stared at the empty display case. "Oh, no!" Ruska cried. "The doll has been stolen! "How could this happen?" Ruska looked all around. "Where is the guard?" she yelled. "He was supposed to watch the doll at all times!"

A tall man rushed over. "I left the doll for only five minutes!" he said.

"What am I going to do?" Ruska cried. "Wait a minute," she added, staring at Ashley and me. "I recognize you two. You're those twin detectives, right?"

Ashley nodded. "I'm Ashley Olsen, and this is my sister, Mary-Kate."

"I need you to find the doll—fast!" Ruska said. "Before my boss discovers it's missing. Or he'll fire me—and the guard, too!"

"I think we should help her," I whispered to Ashley. "I think we should take the case."

Ashley nodded, then turned to Ruska. "How do you think someone got the doll out of the display case?"

That was a good question. I studied the case. It wasn't broken. And it was still locked.

"I don't know!" Ruska said. "But you have to find that doll! It was owned by Princess Anna herself. It's very valuable!"

Ruska was right about that. I read all about the doll in a magazine. It was worth millions!

I circled the display case. There had to be clues around here, somewhere.

I looked behind the case—nothing. I looked on one side of the case—nothing. I looked on the other side. Hey! What was that? I bent down to take a closer peek. Little orange-colored cards were lying on the floor. "Ashley," I whispered, "I found something!"

Ashley hurried over. "They're ticket stubs-- to the movie premiere!"

I picked them up and studied them. "This is our first clue," I said.

"Who could have dropped these here?" Ashley asked.

"I know!" I exclaimed. "Only one person would have a whole stack of ticket stubs. That crabby ticket taker!"

"She's definitely our first suspect," Ashley said. "We'd better go talk to her."

"Yeah," I agreed. "But before we do that, let's look around here a little more."

I got down on my hands and knees. I searched all around. "Ashley!" I cried. "You're not going to believe what I just found!"

Two Times the Fun!
Two Times the Excitement!
Two Times the Adventure!

Check Out All Six *You're Invited* Video Titles...

...And All Four Feature-Length Movies!

And Look for Mary-Kate & Ashley's Adventure Video Series.

DUALSTAR VIDEO

Listen To Us!

Ballet Party™

Birthday Party™

Sleepover Party™

Mary-Kate & Ashley's Cassettes and CDs
Available Now Wherever Music is Sold

It doesn't matter if you live around the corner…
or around the world…
If you are a fan of Mary-Kate and Ashley Olsen,
you should be a member of

MARY-KATE + ASHLEY'S FUN CLUB™

Here's what you get:
Our Funzine™
An autographed color photo
Two black & white individual photos
A full size color poster
An official **Fun Club**™ membership card
A **Fun Club**™ school folder
Two special **Fun Club**™ surprises
A holiday card
Fun Club™ collectibles catalog
Plus a **Fun Club**™ box to keep everything in

To join Mary-Kate + Ashley's Fun Club™, fill out the form
below and send it along with

U.S. Residents – $17.00
Canadian Residents – $22 U.S. Funds
International Residents – $27 U.S. Funds

MARY-KATE + ASHLEY'S FUN CLUB™
859 HOLLYWOOD WAY, SUITE 275
BURBANK, CA 91505

NAME:_____

ADDRESS:_____

CITY:_____ STATE:_____ ZIP:_____

PHONE: (____) _____ BIRTHDATE:_____